Reasons
and
Raisins

J
ALD
cop. 1

by Josephine and Richard Aldridge
illustrated by John Larrecq

PARNASSUS PRESS BERKELEY, CALIFORNIA

to John Albert
and Elizabeth Melissa

"Don't eat the raisins,"
said Mrs. Fox to Little Fox.
"Too much of anything will make you sick."
The real reason she said not to was that
she meant to make raisin pudding for dinner.

But Little Fox was going off on his bike
down Meadow Road
and he wanted some raisins for lunch.
So he took the whole box,
and nobody knew.

Pretty soon he came to Crow.

"Will you give me a ride today?" asked Little Fox.

"What've you got to pay me with?" replied Crow.

"A box of raisins?" said Little Fox.

"Okay, hop on, let's go," said Crow.

Little Fox hid his bike behind a bush
and hopped on.

They flew over a fair.

Crow saw the Fat Lady in front of her tent.

He laughed out loud, "Caw-caw."

The box of raisins dropped from his beak.

"Bosh," said Crow. "Too bad," said Little Fox.

"Too bad for you, too," said Crow.
He tipped his wings
and Little Fox slid off his back.

Little Fox fell and fell
and landed on the Fat Lady's lap.
"Quite a day," said the Fat Lady.
"First a box of raisins, then a fox."

The magician at the next booth
could hardly believe his eyes.
He called over to the Fat Lady,
"Say, Esmerelda, would you like to
have dinner with me tonight?
Here we've had booths side by side all this time
and we barely know each other."
The real reason he asked
was that he wanted to find out
how Esmerelda could have
nothing in her lap one minute
and a box of raisins and a fox the next.
What a neat trick!

The Fat Lady was thrilled.

Nobody had ever asked her to dinner before.

But she called back, "Thank you just the same,

but I have to eat here tonight."

The real reason she said, "No, thank you,"

was that she was ashamed

to let anyone know what size dinner

she usually had.

Last night, for instance, she had gulped down

      one gallon of noodle soup,

      seventeen hamburgers,

      a pound of peas,

      nine baked potatoes,

      two bowls of salad,

      and four quarts of chocolate ice cream.

And by bedtime she had been hungry again.

Little Fox was so interested in the fair
he was willing to stay in the Fat Lady's lap
and let his ears be rubbed.
He saw her put the box of raisins in her bag.
She would have eaten them in one mouthful
except that she wasn't allowed to eat on the job.
She was supposed to introduce herself to people
and talk to them and, every now and then,
recite a poem called "The Fat Poem."

The Fat Poem

As a child I was thin and glum
Though I ate and I ate and I ate
Instead of sucking my thumb.

I snacked on baboons
And sausage balloons
And followed them down with two bibs.

That bunch of baboons
Blew up the balloons
And danced on my tickly ribs.

The bibs tore in half
When I started to laugh –
The baboons all fell down in a heap.

I kept them quiet
With a purple punch diet
And hiccoughed them loudly to sleep.

So look at me now –
Twice the size of a cow
And jolly and fat as they come!

"Pretty soon I have my dinner break,"
the Fat Lady said to Little Fox,
"and we can go into my tent
where I want you to meet Foghorn, my pet dog."
The real reason she wanted them to meet
was that Foghorn was a foxhound
and what he liked to eat more than anything else
was fox.
The Fat Lady carried Little Fox into her tent.
Foghorn woke up from a nap,
took one look at Little Fox,
let out his special blast of a bark,

and jumped straight at him.
But Little Fox wasn't there.
He was out through the tent flap
running for dear life
and caught round his neck like a collar
was the Fat Lady's handbag
with the raisins bumping and rattling inside.

He scooted out under the main gate
and bounded along the curvy up-and-down road.
He kept one ear turned forward,
and one ear turned backward,
listening for Foghorn's voice.

"Stick 'em up!" another voice blurted out.

A masked weasel had jumped out from the bushes
and was blocking the road.

Little Fox skidded to a stop.

"Hand over that purse!" ordered Weasel.

Little Fox did, and Weasel began pawing through it.

"Here, you can have these, I don't want 'em,"
said Weasel, tossing the box of raisins
to Little Fox.

The real reason he gave them back was that
he was only interested in the dollar bills
stuffed in the bottom of the bag.

Just then Foghorn came tearing around the corner.

"Got to get a wiggle on!" said Weasel,

and rushed into the bushes.

Little Fox popped down a hole, pooped.

Foghorn chased off after Weasel

and the Fat Lady's handbag.

Little Fox's hole turned out to be a tunnel.
He burrowed along and along
and after a while came up into daylight again.
There was Meadow Road –
and there was his bike behind the bush!
He climbed on and headed home.

Little Fox walked into the kitchen
where Mrs. Fox was working on supper.
"Hi, Mom," he said, "I'm home. Sorry I'm late."
"Hi," said Mrs. Fox.
"Have you seen the raisins by any chance?"
"Why, here they are right here," said Little Fox.

"I kept them safe all day
and didn't eat a single one
because you didn't want me to."
The real reason he said that
was that he didn't want to be scolded
for doing something he shouldn't have done.

"Thank you," said Mrs. Fox. "Now come here!"
And she caught Little Fox and spanked him.
She didn't want him to know
she had seen Crow flying over
with a red furry tail flowing out behind.

They had raisin pudding for supper after all –
"to give the raisins a rest," said Mrs. Fox.
But the real reason was that

she knew it was Little Fox's favorite dessert,
and she was more glad than she could say
that he was safely home.

2.